MW00899386

Maurice meets the Polly Wog

By Jeannaka Andrews

This book is dedicated to my children.
Never forget to pray.
Love Mommy

It had been a long day for Maurice and his Mommy. She had run a lot of errands before returning home to prepare dinner. As she pulled into the driveway Mommy said, "Okay Maurice are you ready to go in and get dinner started? I'm making your favorite." Mommy pulled into the driveway and turned off the car.

Maurice sat patiently in his car seat and played with his toy train as she unloaded the grocery bags into the house, "Toot Too!

All of a sudden, it appeared on the windshield of Mommy's car. Maurice's eyes grew large with excitement. "POLLY POG!" He yelled with enthusiasm trying to get out of his car seat. He was bouncing up and down. "SEE MOMMY, SEE! A POLLY WOG!" Mommy quickly unsecured his seat belt.

"Let's get you unbuckled," she said because Maurice just wouldn't be still. "Mommy, Polly Wog," he said in amazement.

"I'm hungry too. Let's go get dinner started", Mommy said to him. She thought he was hungry and anxious to eat dinner, but the last thing on Maurice's mind was food. He looked for the Polly Wog, but there was nothing there.
"POOF!"
It was gone.

"How about a snack while I get dinner started?" Besides his toy train, snacks were his favorite and Mommy always shared the best snacks. She gave him chocolate chip cookies that were shaped like little animals to enjoy as he sat in his chair. They tasted so good and made his stomach so happy.

While enjoying his cookies, he looked out the window, and there it was again sitting on the windowsill.

"POLLY WOG! MOMMY SEE! He was pointing toward the window.
Maurice was so excited. He was moving all around in his high chair
trying to get down.
"MAURICE!" Mommy exclaimed as she quickly ran toward the high chair
so that it didn't topple over with him in it.
 "POLLY WOG, MOMMY SEE!" When Mommy looked in the direction he
was pointing, there was nothing there.
"POOF!"
It was gone.

Maurice was sad and disappointed. He thought his Mommy didn't believe him. After dinner, Maurice went to find his older sister Maya. He started babbling on and on about what he'd seen. He was filled with so much enthusiasm. He was talking so fast that she couldn't make heads or tails of what he was talking about so, she decided to tell him about her day at school instead.

She started twirling and dancing as she talked about how fabulous her day was. She was in the *Kindergarten* now, which meant she was a 'BIG' girl. Maurice kept on and on trying to tell her about the Polly Wog, but she wasn't listening to him. She was only interested in showing him the new dance she'd learned from her cool friends at school.

Maurice left Maya to her dancing and walked into the living room where he saw his Grandmee. She was holding his baby sister Jeaniah. Grandmee watched her during the day while Mommy and Daddy worked and the kids went to school. Maurice thought for sure that Grandmee would listen to him. She always listened to him.

"Hey there Maurice. Why the long face?" Grandmee said.
Just as he started to tell her about the Polly Wog, Jeaniah started to cry really loud. "Oh my! Give Grandmee a minute to calm her down, then my ears are all yours" she said.

Maurice gave a big sigh, dropped his shoulders, and walked away leaving Grandmee to tend to Jeaniah. Nobody believes me he thought.

Maurice found Daddy outside. "Why the long face Sport? I know what will turn your frown upside down," Daddy said and grabbed the soccer ball. Daddy rolled it to him and he kicked it back to him with all his might. Maurice loved playing ball with Daddy. His Daddy was so much fun. He thought his Daddy was the strongest and bravest person in the world. Daddy rolled the ball to Maurice again and he missed it.

"That's okay little buddy, you'll get it next time", Daddy always had a way of making him feel like he could do anything. Maurice, all smiles and giggles, ran to get the ball that he'd missed.

He was so excited when he found it by the bush. He bent down to pick it up and to his surprise, there it was again.
Maurice screamed exuberantly, DADDY, POLLY WOG SEE!"

Maurice ran back to Daddy and grabbed his hand to pull him toward the direction the ball rolled. Daddy ran quickly behind Maurice not sure what he was looking for. "Polly Wog?" Daddy said to himself.

When he got to the bush, there was nothing there. Daddy didn't see anything. Again, Maurice's heart was so sad. He wanted desperately to show his Daddy the Polly Wog. He knew for sure that if Daddy saw it, he would help him tell Mommy and Maya about it.

Mommy would be so proud of him for finding it. Maya would think he was super cool like the kids at her school because he had a Polly Wog.

When they reached the bush, there was nothing there.
"POOF!"
It was gone.

During bath time, all Maurice could talk about was the Polly Wog. He was rambling on and on about the Polly Wog as Mommy tried to get him into his pj's. Mommy just couldn't understand what he was talking about and she felt so sad for him. She could tell that he was getting frustrated trying to explain what was on his mind with his two-year-old vocabulary.

"Don't worry", she reassured him. "I'm sure that I'll see it next time". Mommy tried to ease his little mind from frustration, but it didn't help. "You'll feel better after a good night's sleep." Maurice was too excited to sleep.

It was time to say prayers and go to bed. Everyone gathered in Maurice's room and knelt down at his bed. Mommy sat on his bed with Jeaniah. Daddy tried to calm him down from such an eventful day. Maya knelt next to Daddy and then everyone put their hands together like a teepee tent to pray. Finally, everyone closed their eyes and said their prayers together:

"Now I lay me, down to sleep,

I Pray the Lord my soul to keep.

May angels watch me through the night,

and wake me with the morning light.

Amen"

Mommy and Daddy tucked the kids in and kissed them good night, but all Maurice could think about was the Polly Wog. He tossed and turned until he eventually fell sound asleep. "Polly Wog, ZZZZ!"

The next morning, after everyone was all ready to start their day, Mommy gathered the kids' backpacks for school. Jeaniah had to stay with Grandmee. She was too little to go to school.

"Ok kids let's go. Tell Daddy you'll see him later." Daddy gave them all kisses and hugs as he left for work. The kids piled in Mommy's car. Maya helped Maurice fasten his car seat and then fastened her seat belt.

"BUCKLES!" The kids sang out in unison to let Mommy know they were secure in their seat belts. Maya started singing to the radio. Mommy started to back out the driveway and there it was. Suddenly, there it was. "POLLY WOG! SEE MAYA! SEE MOMMY! Maurice pointed at the porch. Mommy turned and looked and there it was. Maya looked at the porch and started bouncing in her seat. "I see it, Maurice. I see it!" Oh boy, he thought. They can see it! They can REALLY see it!

Mommy quickly put the car in park. Maya helped Maurice unfasten his seat belt after she'd removed hers. They jumped out of the car and raced to the porch. Mommy met them there. "My Polly Wog! See Mommy. See Maya." Maurice was so excited that finally, he was able to show them his mysterious friend, the Bull Frog.

CPSIA information can be obtained
at www.ICGtesting.com
Printed in the USA
BVHW021426281021
620172BV00005B/261

9 781087 901664